KU-543-949

Withdrawn from stock

For Xavi Narwhal and Bodhi Narwhal,
with love Auntie Fiyaz – EA

For the most supportive grandma in the shire,
love always x – KH

Emma Adams and Katy Halford

# Naughty Narwhal

SCHOLASTIC

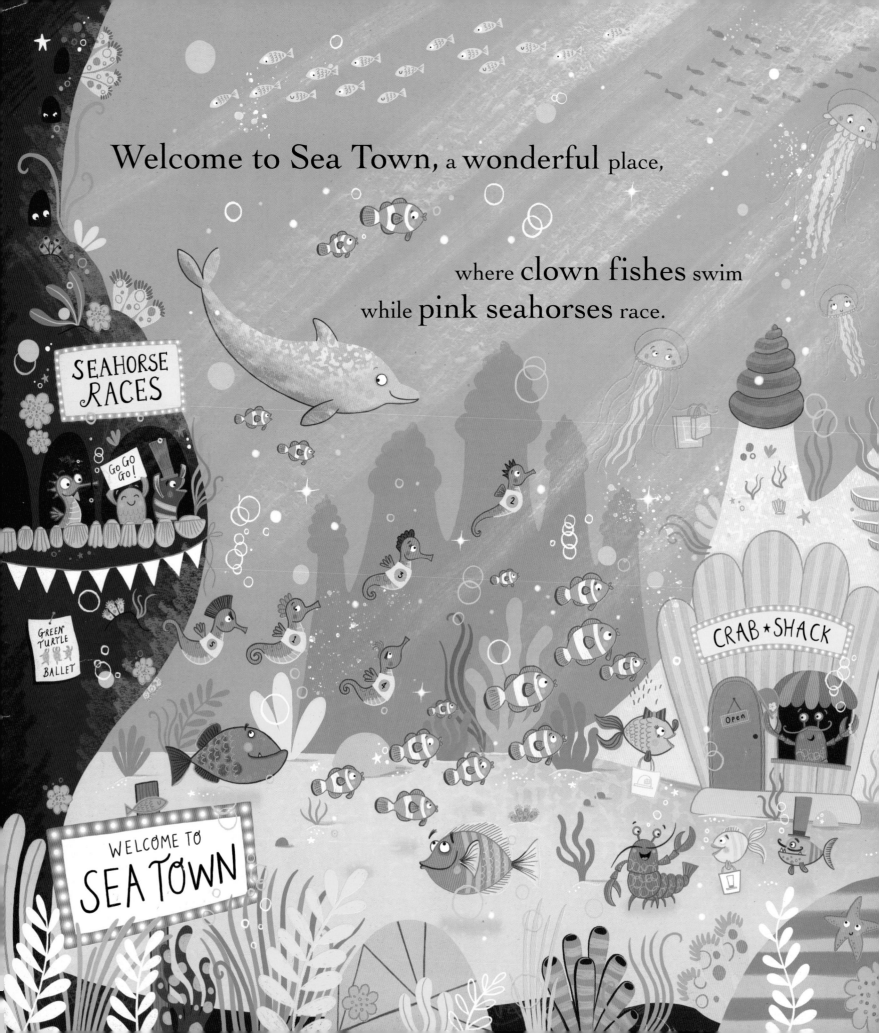

Welcome to Sea Town, a wonderful place,

where clown fishes swim
while pink seahorses race.

SEAHORSE
RACES

GO GO
GO!

GREEN
TURTLE
BALLET

CRAB ★ SHACK

Open

WELCOME TO
SEA TOWN

OCTOPUS HEIGHTS

The green turtles dance, and an octopus swings

FISH FOOD GRILL

FIN GLAM

near lobsters that lay while a puffer fish stings.

OUCH!

Everyone's friends here, they love to have fun.
That is, every creature except for . . .

. . . this one.

YIKES!

BEWARE
NAUGHTY NARWHAL

Meet Naughty Narwhal – here she is, right on cue.
She's simply the **naughtiest** narwhal, it's true!

You never would guess all that she has in store,
but, listen, come closer, and I'll tell you more . . .

One sunny day, in the deepest blue sea,
Narwhal was feeling as **bored as can be.**
Distractedly, she swam along the seabed,
and that's when she spied her friend $\text{Crab}$ up ahead.

Hiding behind the tall seagrass that grew,

she waited . . .

and waited . . .

and then cried out . . .

"BOO!"

Next thing you know, with a glint in her eye,
Narwhal saw **Jellyfish** swishing nearby.

Before anyone had the chance to say STOP,
she pointed her horn, then took aim
and went,

POP!

HEY!

How Narwhal giggled
and chuckled with glee,
until she heard something –
now what could it be . . . ?

LA LA LA

Cookies, cakes, sandwiches, all in a row.

A party!

5 TODAY!

Was Narwhal invited . . . ?
OH NO.

No one had asked her – no, they hadn't said.
So what happened next?

And off Narwhal swam, with an unhappy swish,
along the bright coral, past kelp and starfish.

Deeper

and deeper

Ahhh!

through seagrass that swayed,
as shadows appeared and the light seemed to fade.

Until . . .

There in the dark
sat a **weathered shipwreck**,

with a mast pointing **high**
on a **large wooden deck.**

She jumped with surprise as she heard a loud creak.

What was inside?
She would just take a peek . . .

Inside the ship,
Narwhal went to explore

and look at the treasures
that lay on the floor.

She felt a bit sad –
oh, her friends had been cross.

But she wasn't sorry –
yes, she was the boss!

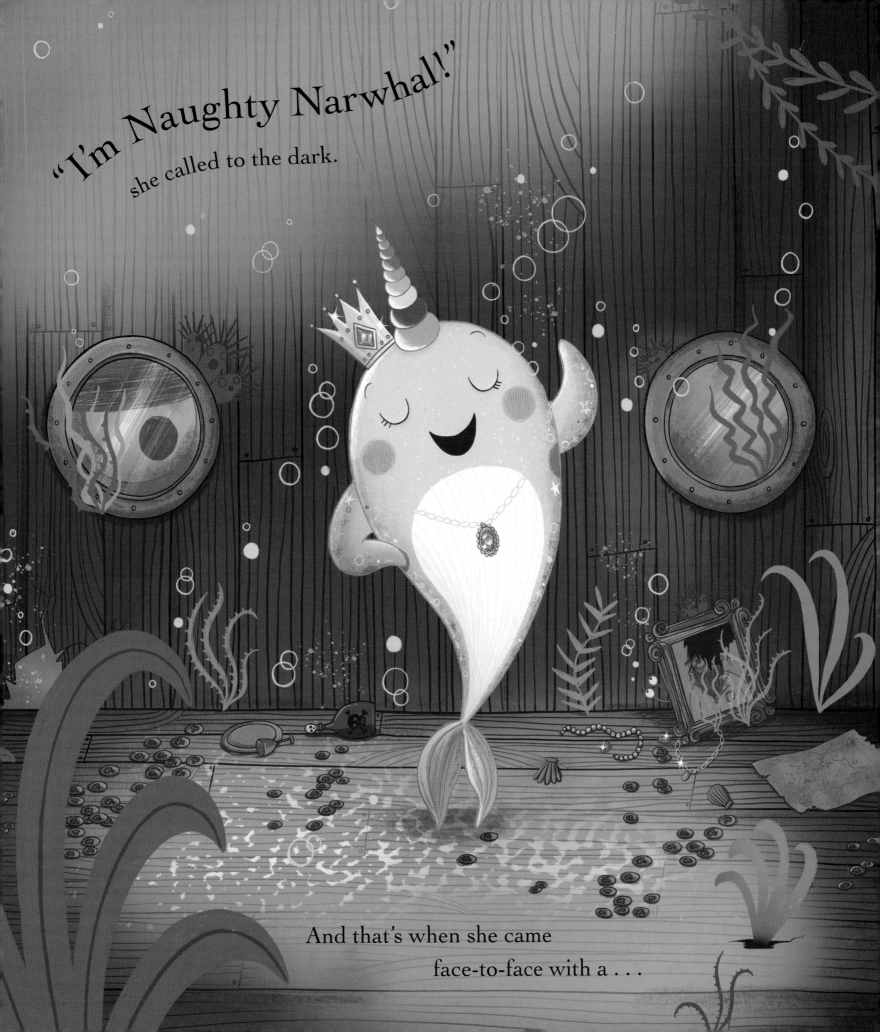

"I'm Naughty Narwhal!" she called to the dark.

And that's when she came
face-to-face with a . . .

. . . shark!

"Help!" whispered Narwhal, so scared and afraid,
but do you think **anyone** came to her aid?

Of course not!

For this naughty, rude, teeny-weenie,
had been such a ghastly
and naughty **big meanie.**

The **shark** looked at her, and she looked up at him.
There was nothing left for it, she just had to . . .

# . . . SWIM!

Out of the shipwreck,

and up to the town,

she swam through the coral and didn't slow down.

Then sped to her bedroom and into her bed,
and pulled all the covers right over her head!

Poor little Narwhal, so terribly sad –
her naughty behaviour was terribly bad.

How could she fix things – was there a way?
If only there was **something** that she could say.

Suddenly Narwhal knew just what to do.
She leapt out of bed and then – **weee!** – off she flew.

Back in the town every lobster, crab, fish
was at the **Crab Shack**
(oh, that place is **SO** swish).

Narwhal **burst** in
and they **gasped** in surprise
(she made Lobster jump –
he tipped over his fries!).

She stayed at the front so that they could all see,
then said, "I'm so sorry,
oh, please forgive me!"

Would they forgive her?
She did seem sincere.

Well, finally everyone gave a big . . .

For they knew the **one thing**
that **everyone** should –

it was never too late
to decide to be good.

And there with her friends, having fun on the reef,
Narwhal agreed to turn over a new leaf.

After that day, Narwhal played **no more** pranks.
She was **super-nice** – always said **please** and **thanks**.

Naughty no more, she was **happy as can be,**
in this wonderful place in the deepest blue sea,
where all creatures smile and they love to have fun.

That is, every creature **including** this one.

First published in 2019 by Scholastic Children's Books
This edition published in 2020 by Scholastic Children's Books
Euston House, 24 Eversholt Street
London NW1 1DB
a division of Scholastic Ltd
www.scholastic.co.uk
London – New York – Toronto – Sydney – Auckland
Mexico City – New Delhi – Hong Kong

Text copyright © Emma Adams 2019
Illustrations copyright © Katy Halford 2019
PB ISBN  978 0702 30357 9
C&F ISBN 978 1407 19628 2

All rights reserved
Printed in China

1 3 5 7 9 10 8 6 4 2

The moral rights of Emma Adams and Katy Halford have been asserted.

Papers used by Scholastic Children's Books are made
from wood grown in sustainable forests.